To Robert —

You are by far one of the
best people I have
ever met.

Thank you for your
support brother

FOCUS WRITE INSPIRE. LLC

8
Days
In
A
Week

SERRON

Copyright © 2008 by Serron Green

8 DAYS IN A WEEK

Written by SERRON

Edited by ESHAM ABDUL GILES

Cover Design by BAJA UKWELI

For further information about this book, write all inquires and permissions to;

Focus Write Inspire LLC.

PO BOX 373

NEWARK, NJ 07101

www.FocusWriteInspire.com

Library of Congress Cataloging-in-Publication Data is available.

Library of Congress Control Number: 2013954798

ISBN-13: 978-0-615-91807-5

DEDICATION

To my Dad: I love you and miss you. Without you, there would be no me. I know you're watching. Mom: I love you more than you will ever know. My brothers: Malek and Sabu: We're brothers for life. I love ya'll cats. Breezy: Daddy loves you so much, and you're crazy momma too. LOL. Sam, Rameck, and Geroge: Keep doing what you're doing! The kids need you. If ever you need my help, holla! Meca, and Tash: You guys are the best. Without you, this would not have been possible. Thank you. I mean that! And to everyone who thought that I could when I thought that I could not.

And last but certainly not least, God… for giving me all the gifts that you have given me. I love my life and wouldn't trade it for anything in the world.

I thank you.

8
Days
In
A
Week

PREFACE

What's up y'all? My name is Isaac Jordan. (Pronounced Isaiah) I would say for the most part, "I am your average man." I like sports, beer and women. Just like any other guy. I only hang out with a couple of close friends. Mekhi and Sun, these two brothers are my best friends. We all are the same in many ways, but I think it is our differences that keep us tight. Mekhi is one of those smooth, cool, kind of guys, his style alone gets him over. He usually goes after the women that haven't seen too much. Sun on the other hand, tends to go for the women who get caught up in that "Oooo, he's got a nice body tight shirt shit." Now me, I like women...All of them! Sometimes I wish that pussy came on shelves like canned goods in the supermarket. That way you wouldn't have to be bothered with the extra piece of meat around the pussy. Like I said, I am your average guy. But I also know that my cronies and I are different from every other man in the sense that we love women. And when I say that we love women, I don't mean like other guys who go crazy when they see a fine woman, they lose their mind and their cool...some of the things that happen to us, those cheese ball muthafuckas' couldn't even imagine happening to them. Trust Me! I mean, as far as women go, they're like a job to us...It's what we do. Now I would have to admit that we may take women for granted. And we most definitely mistreat them knowing we are dead wrong. But life is unfair... And so are we. Now I don't want you to think that we just run around fucking every woman over or fucking every single one that we see, although the end part of that would be nice it's not reality. You have to realize this, at one point in time, we were all good men. Then we found out that women don't seem to appreciate the good wholesome nice guy muthafuckas'. So we made a pact between us that we would let no woman put us under. Not one! Meaning, all that chasing women shit is for the birds. We live by a set of rules that regular cats can't possibly understand. All that taking you out all the time to eat shit, NOT! All that calling you all the time shit, NOT! And most importantly, we maintain our dignity with women at all cost. Our mindset is, US first, who cares what the women think. I mean, there are times when I feel like I want to be in a relationship, who wouldn't? But the drama that I see other cats going through doesn't outweigh being free and unattached. The shit they do! Shit like: "Where have you been?" "Who were you with?" Don't need none of that condom counting, rummaging through my shit when I leave them alone in my space, or bitching and moaning about not spending enough time with them or all that other bullshit, their extra fucking baggage and circumstances that you have to put up with in a structured relationship…FUCK THAT! Now it may seem like I am a bit hostile towards women. And I am. I guess you could say that I've had my heart broken. But shit happens. It's just that I would prefer for the shit to happen to someone else. Once I heard that players are born. Well, I think they're born and made. Of course some cats are born with good looks, like me. The gift of gab, like me. A lot of money, not like me. But I do alright. Now you can be born with any of those things, but you can't be born with the desire to want to do women wrong. Besides, who needs a big Benz when you got a big dick?

To a certain extent you have to be motivated. And this is what makes for a dangerous Man Whore. Motivation is the key to being a successful He-Bitch. That and having no remorse will take you a long damn way in the pursuit of flesh. That aspect of pillaging is learned over a period of time. So, I would like to take you on a journey, from Saturday to Saturday, in my life, hence the title *Eight Days in a Week*. Now you might like it. Then again you might not, especially, my women. Sorry ladies, but that's just the way it is. And fellas practice your craft and attack your job with vigor. I hope you have fun while you're with me. I know I will.

CONTENTS

Disclaimer

Some names and identifying details have been changed to protect the privacy of individuals. This is a work of fiction. Names, characters, businesses, places, events and incidents are either the products of the author's imagination or used in a fictitious manner. Any resemblance to actual persons, living or dead, or actual events is purely coincidental.

SATURDAY

"KNOCK, KNOCK, KNOCK!"

I open my eyes and roll over to look at the bright red lights from the digital clock. It reads 9:45pm. Who could that be? Everyone knew that I wasn't going to be home; at least that's what I thought.

"Who's that boo?" comes from the warm body cuddled up against mine. This night, it happens to be Lisa. She's my Spanish mami, 5'6", about 130 lbs. Lots of attitude, your typical feisty Puerto Rican Woman. Rose colored skin, long straight reddish blonde hair, she has a thick deep voice and some very serious hip action. I've been dealing with her for about seven months off and on since we met at the rink at a kiddie party for one of my boy's kids. All I can say about her is this: very, very aggressive. That's what draws me to her. The fact that she seems to need and want to fuck the shit out of me all the time doesn't hurt either.

"KNOCK, KNOCK, KNOCK!"

This time the knocks were even louder. I sighed out loud hoping that whoever it was would go away. But as soon as I closed my eyes, the knocking starts again. "Shit! It's probably one of my brother's wild ass friends looking for him," My brother Malek and I share a basement apartment for the time being. Whenever someone came over they would bang on the damn window right outside of my bedroom if they saw the hallway light on. I got up, slipped on some sweats and a t-shirt and staggered to the door. I always felt like I had been in a fight whenever Lisa came by. When I finally made it to the door I was ready to curse somebody's ass out. Leaving Lisa's warm body was something that I didn't take kindly too .

I looked through the peephole and didn't see anyone at first. "Good," I thought. Maybe they had left before I got to the door. Just as I was about to walk away, a face popped up in my line of sight. "Hey You." My eyes opened so wide they could have lit up the night sky. It was Sada. "SURPRISE!" she said, full of all kinds of giddiness. Surprise was right. This bitch lived at least three hours and three train rides away. What the fuck is she doing here? Especially unannounced? I backed away from the door hoping that maybe this was not happening. My heart was beating so fast I thought that I was about to go into cardiac arrest. Ok, now I have to stay cool. I'm going to have to use all the slick talking and fast thinking that I've practiced and perfected over all my years of being trifling. I quickly scurried down the hall like the rat bastard that I was to my bedroom.

By now Lisa was sitting up wide awake with a pair of my boxers on. She looked good like that, particularly with her hair dangling down over her supple breasts. Unfortunately I could not endeavor into her Spanish dish right now.

"Who's that!?" Lisa said rather suspiciously.

"Oh that's just one of my brother's cronies, Omar," I said as casual as possible considering my current situation. "I'm just going to step outside and talk to him for a minute, I'll be right back." I turned around and strolled out the door. As soon as I hit the hallway I hauled ass down the hall to the stairs that led to the outside door. I looked through the peephole again, took a deep breath and opened the door. And there she was, in all her natural splendor. Sada was built pretty much like Lisa. I just preferred that body type. But she was definitely different. Her complexion was a rich brown tone, almost like roasted almonds. Her eyes were round and full. Her lips...mmm, her lips, just seeing them made me get a chubby. I met her at one of those Freak Nic things last summer in Atlanta. Because of the fact that she went to Penn

State, I never expected her to just show up like this all the way in Jersey. She was smart, fine as hell, and spoke more than one language. The latter being what I always looked for. We had been dating for awhile, so like most women who date a man for awhile, she started assuming that there was more to our relationship than there actually was. It was easy to make it seem that way since she lived so far away. She really thought that I was her boyfriend or something. Women are so fucking stupid sometimes.

When she came in, she kissed me on my right cheek just like she always did. My thoughts were so frantic that I wasn't really sure what to do, so I just escorted her to the living room and tried to sound like I was happy to see her.

"So what are you doing here?" I asked.

"I just thought that I would surprise you," she replied.

"Surprise!" Surprise is an understatement," I said sarcastically under my breath. That is when I gathered myself and started with the bullshit. "I wish you had called, I was just about to go out the door when you knocked. I was on my way to Manhattan for drinks with the fellas. As a matter of fact, they're already on their way over here." But of course that's not exactly what was going to happen. I remembered that my brother and his friends were going out. So I figured if anything I would just go with them, take Sada with me, and just leave Lisa in my bedroom. Of course she would get angry and then leave. I would have to patch things up later. "Look I'm about to leave right now, I'm gonna get a jacket and I'll be right back." I walked away casually, but as soon as I got out of her sight I bolted down the stairs and went back into the bedroom. Time must have been flying by because when I opened the door Lisa already had her clothes on.

"What the fuck took you so long?" she said with so much fire I could feel the heat from her breath.

"I told you that I was going to talk to one of my brother's friends and lost track of time." Her eyes were filled with all kinds of anger as she watched me walk across the room and pick up an old army jacket lying across my bed.

"Now where are you going? I ain't gonna be waitin' for you all night." Her Hispanic accent started to become heavier. She was beginning to become a little antsy.

"I want to leave!" She blurted out.

Just relax, I'm not going to leave you here for a long time," I said. There is no way I can let Lisa see Sada. They had only heard about each other once before, Lisa called and for some reason Sada decided to answer the phone. Very bad scene. In a fight Lisa would kill Sada, and I really wanted no part of that in my house.

"I'm just going to give this jacket to him. It's gotten a little chilly since you got here and he said that he didn't feel like going all the way home to get something to put on."

She huffed. "Ok, but you better hurry the fuck up."

Whew! Feisty as hell and I loved it. I go back down the hall, up the stairs to the living room. Sada was much more patient with the delay than Lisa had been. She lay kicked back on the couch with her shoes off. "SHOES OFF!!!" bellowed out in my head.

"Put your shoes on!" Spewed out of my mouth without me even thinking.

She sat up slowly, put her shoes back on and said, "Why are you so testy?"

"I'm just in a hurry, let's go!"

"I wanted to relax for a minute; it is a little chilly out."

Now my head is starting to hurt, she's got me thinking that she can feel how close I am to a panic attack. "They're waiting for me and you know that I don't like to have people waiting for me."

"Ok, Ok, could you at least get me a jacket or something to put on?"

Now I have to go back down stairs and get another jacket, Lisa is going to find that strange for sure. The only thing is that there is really no reply for what she said so around the corner and back down the stairs into the room.

Lisa was enraged. "I'm getting the fuck outta here right now!" She stormed past me faster than I could react, I tried to grab her, but all the working out that she did made her a little stronger than I expected. I caught her from behind and spun her around.

"Would you just go and sit down, I'll be with you in a minute." I said it in a tone hoping it would make her understand that I was not playing. Instead she erupted like Mt. Saint Helens. She pushed away from me and screamed out something in Spanish. I don't think that I would want to know what it was anyway. Just as fast as she spoke she darted down the hall. I'm not sure what happened next, but I lost my footing when I grabbed her and "BAM" we were on the floor at the bottom of the stairway. She was struggling to get all my weight off of her.

"Get the fuck off me!" She yelled. I somehow got to my feet as she scrambled to get away, then that's when shit got hectic.

"Isaac', what the heck is going on?"

I looked up thinking that it was Sada. As my eyes focused, all I could do is let out was an exasperated, "Mom." My mother was standing at the top of the stairs. Her 5-foot frame was stunned by the sight of me holding Lisa in a headlock on the floor. Mom stopped by from time to time to check on my brother and me. Unfortunately, this was one of those times.

"Nothing's going on," I said flatly. Lisa stopped struggling, maybe because she was tired or maybe because she wanted to show Mom Dukes some respect. Nonetheless, she just stopped. I think my mom must have had an idea of what was going on because she just accepted my answer and moved away from the top of the stairs. I took Lisa by the hand and led her back to the bedroom. In a gentle tone I said, "You go first." As soon as she went into the bedroom I slammed the door and locked it from the outside. As I went down the hall I could hear her cursing and banging on the door like a ravenous dog. I just ignored it and made my way back up the stairs.

By now Sada was restless as hell; I could see the irritation on her face. "Who's here Isaac'?"

"Nobody," I quickly replied. Her facial expression changed from soft to hurt just as quickly as I answered. I could tell she knew I was lying, but the rules of the game say: "Never admit to anything."

"Who's here?" she repeated. This time her voice cracked as her eyes filled with tears. That moment broke me. Seeing her fall apart like that hurt. As bad as I am, I do have some feelings. "Lisa," I replied. Tears streamed down her face.

"I want to see her."

"What?"

"I said I want to see her. "Now!"

The tone of her voice didn't sit well with me, even if I was the one that was wrong. "Look, take your ass in the living room and sit down." At least this time the tone in my voice worked. She went and plopped down on the couch.

"I'm sorry about this, but you're so far away I get tired of being alone sometimes."

Either this girl is stupid or she was so blown away by the fact that I had the balls to say some bullshit like that.

She leaned forward, "I want to go home."

I will admit to being a bit confused for a second but this was my opportunity to get rid of her ass. I grabbed the phone, called a cab and sat silent. It felt like her eyes were burning through my skin when she looked at me. Finally I heard the cab horn. "Taxi's here." She stood up, put on the army jacket, picked up her bag and headed to the door. When she got to the door she stopped in front of me, I didn't have a clue as to what was about to happen, but I was on the defensive.

"Money. Enough to get home."

Her voice was cold as winter. But at this point I would do anything to end this. I pulled out my wallet and gave her a fifty. "That should get you home."

"Whatever muthefucka," she replied.

I opened the door and she went out. As soon as she went out of the door, I closed it. Everything was starting to come back under control. All I had to do now was talk some sweetness to Lisa and everything would at least be straight with her and me. It didn't make sense to lose them both, besides, good dick always helped.

When I got back to the bedroom door it was quiet. Again I had that unsure feeling overcome me. I put the key in the door slowly, as if it had been wired by a Tony Soprano underling, set to explode when I turned the knob. I opened the door and entered with some serious caution. Unlike Sada, Lisa might attack me. Instead Lisa was sitting on the bed massaging her temples like she had the mother of all headaches.

"I'm going to tell you the truth before you even ask. That was someone that I use to deal with that I'm having a problem getting rid of." Straight up lies. She was quiet for about 20 seconds, then she raised her head slowly, her long hair hung down in her face, the stress of the situation was all over her face.

"I just want to go."

I pushed opened the door and gestured for her to leave. As she walked up the stairs, her steps were heavy and deliberate. As we got to the door, she stopped and turned to me.

"I knew it had to be a woman."

I never in my wildest dreams thought that she had genuine feelings for me until that moment. This was a side of her I had never seen before. I could see the hurt in her eyes. I could feel that she wanted to say more, but didn't. Besides, I needed to be alone. I opened the door and let the chilly night air come in. As I stepped out onto the porch something felt strange about the outside air. I could feel someone peering at me through the darkness. I stood motionless in the cold night air and used my eyes to scan the area outside without moving my head. I noticed movement to my left. Sada!!! This bitch was using the army jacket that I gave her very well. Sada was hiding in the bushes along the side of my house. Lisa noticed me noticing Sada. Sada stepped from the bushes and screamed my name out like a banshee. I was expecting Lisa to lose it.

"Fuck you Isaac'." She said in a low somber voice.

She walked off of the porch glaring at Sada as she walked towards her car. My head was pounding with thoughts of what to do. I sorted through the jumbled thoughts as fast as I could. Suddenly headlights snapped me out of my daze. As soon as the car turned the corner I immediately recognized it. It was my mother and father. As soon as my Pops saw what was going on he didn't even stop. He pulled into the driveway, put the car in reverse, backed out and drove away. As he drove away, Mom looked back at me. She had a look of concern, but I could sense Pops telling her that I was on my own. As they disappeared, I decided to do the same. I strolled off of the porch as if nothing had happened. As I got to the corner I could hear Lisa's car engine revving up. She started to pull off just as I walked across the street. Then all of a sudden I heard tires screeching. I turned around as fast as I could to see what was coming.

"LISA!!!" I yelled out. She swerved onto the wrong side of the street and was trying to run my black ass down. Her eyes were on fire as she sped towards me. I started running as hard and as fast as I could, but that little black car was bearing down on me way too fast. I was about to get killed by a wild Puerto Rican in a little black piece of shit car that didn't look so little anymore. As she came closer, I took a desperate leap out of the street and landed between two parked cars like a pancake. My hands and knees were hurting like a muthafucka.

"Bitch I'm gonna kill you!" are the only words I could muster up.

"Next time I'm gonna kill your black ass," was all I heard from the car as Lisa sped by.

"I can't believe this shit is happening," I mumbled to myself. That chick really tried to hit me, and I can't lie, I was scared to death. My eyes were filled with water from the dirt that flew up when I hit the ground. Then something else hit me. Sada was still standing in front of my house. No time to be hurt now. I got to my feet. Damn, my knees were killing me and my pants were soiled with oil from the ground. I wiped off the best that I could, considering how bad my hands were hurting. I don't think I could take one more thing at this point, I thought. I just put my hands in my pockets and started walking towards the store on the corner.

All that I could think about was Lisa trying to run me down. "Isaac'" I heard my name. "Isaac'" I heard it again. I turned around. "Shit," I guess Sada decided to leave my front porch and follow me. Her eyes were filled with almost every emotion a woman could have. Hate was the one I noticed most. But I was in no mood for her or any other conflict, so I just kept walking. And, so did she. The closer she got, the more insane she looked. Her eyes were wide open, filled with intensity. The thought of her trying to attack me was running through my mind. As she came closer I decided to pick up my pace to put some distance between us. I finally made it to the Chinese restaurant on the corner. When I went into the store I didn't even look back, I just wanted to be in a place where I could see her coming. I waited a few minutes, but she never came in. I decided to take a peek outside to see if she was waiting. I held on to the doorway as I stuck my head out. This way if she grabbed me, she wouldn't be able to pull me out and I wouldn't have to kick her ass. I looked left and then right, I didn't see her. As a matter of fact, I didn't see anyone. There was a very surreal feel about it. There wasn't a soul on the street, not even a car. I stepped out onto the sidewalk and still didn't see her.

"Maybe she went back to the house?" I said to myself. My stomach was in knots and I was standing on the street talking to myself. "Fuck this!!! I think I will meet up with my brother and his friends. I don't need this drama in my life." I started to walk up the slight hill to my brother's people's house, Kevin. Kevin was a friend of my brothers from way back. Very gangsta, but cool. As I walked I started to realize how exhausted I was from the late night's excitement. I was in a total daze until footsteps behind me snapped me out of it. Sada appeared out of thin air like a ghost. "Was she hiding under a car?" The way that it happened really made me nervous. As I got to the driveway of the house that was about four houses from Kevin's, I made a break for it. If this girl was going to get me she was going to have to earn it. I ran up the driveway into the darkness. I grew up around here so I knew that the backyards connected throughout the whole block. I climbed through bushes, sticks, grass and over one wooden fence. There was no way she could have kept up, especially with a backpack on and not knowing where Kevin lived couldn't help either. I ran around the back of his house to the side door and knocked softly so only the people inside could hear. Daryl, Kevin's brother, came to the door and looked through the window.

"What's up chief?" He said.

"Just open the door man, shit is serious out here."

Daryl let me in and we went into the living room.

"What's the matter with you?" He asked.

I told him about the night's events as quickly as I could. Daryl just chuckled at my agony. When I thought about it, it was kind of funny. We sat and talked about the whole thing for about forty-five minutes. Then we heard a car pull up in the driveway as music began to seep through the walls of the house. It was Kevin and Omar. When they came in, they each had a puzzled look on their faces.

"What's up fellas? Y'all look like you had a night like Isaac'." Daryl said.

"There's a girl sitting on the porch staring out into space."

I know this crazy ass girl did not find me. There is no way. We all went to the window and looked out onto the dark porch. Sure enough, it was Sada.

"How the hell did she find me? Does she have radar?" I whispered as we walked back into the living room. "What am I going to do now?"

"You're gonna get that bitch off of my porch, that's what you're going to do," Kevin interrupted before I could say another word. The tone he used was in a joking way, but I knew that he was serious. There was really nothing else left for me to do except go out there and confront her. I did feel reassured because Kevin, Omar and Daryl came out with me. The night air was biting by now, which added to the mystery of Sada suddenly appearing out of nowhere. When she saw us coming towards her, her eyes were fixated on me as if I were alone. And for that moment of eye contact, I was.

"What the fuck. Do you have radar or something?" I screamed. Her look turned black, she was seeing a side of me that she had never seen before. I had always been, for the most part, kind and giving towards her.

13

I quickly turned to Kevin. "Give me your phone," I demanded. I took the phone and dialed the number to the local cab company. You must always have a taxicab number in your mental rolodex in case of an emergency. The cab came in less than five minutes. I walked over to the cab and opened the door. Sada did not move an inch.

"Get in."

"No."

"What?"

"No."

"I'm not playing with you, get in the cab."

"No"

"Look Sada, I'm sorry about what happened, but you gotta go."

The cab driver interrupted, "Is anybody getting in?"

Back and forth we went; still she refused to get in the cab. After about ten minutes, the cab driver yelled, "Close the door!" I glared at him as if this evening was all his doing. I was just so tired from everything that had happened that I closed the door without saying another word.

"Isaac', what are you gonna do?" Kevin inquired. "If you want, we can drop her off at the train station." Kevin jogged up the driveway to get his car.

"Sada, if you do not get in the car I'm going to leave you here." I guess she started to realize the futility of the situation. When Kevin backed up in front of us she got in the back of the car, still speechless. Unfortunately, I had to sit in the back with her. Daryl decided to pass on the ride because of the obvious tension.

The ride was quiet between Sada and I. Kevin and Omar sat up front smoking a blunt and sharing a twenty-two ounce Heineken. The car was filled with smoke within minutes. I figured with all the drama that I might as well partake in the slow suicide. I guzzled down as much beer as I could as fast as I could. As I drank from the bottle, Sada leaned over and started babbling about how she was going to have her brothers kick my ass. But the more she talked, the less I heard. All that I could hear was gibberish. As we drove up in front of the train station, the effects of the beer and the stinky green began to generate a buzz.

"Can I get my money back?" I slurred.

"Are you crazy?" She said in a high-pitched voice. "I catch you with another woman and you have the nerve to ask for your money back."

I paused for a couple seconds because what she said made sense. "Yes... I do." I stated without hostility or malice. Her face softened. Maybe she had had enough. I don't know, but she took the fifty out and crumbled it up and tossed it towards me. As she got out of the car, I stared at her sweet ass as if I would never see it again.

Later on that night when I came in, I called Lisa and then Sada. I made up some crap about how much I would miss each of them and how the other wasn't shit and didn't mean anything to me. Reminded them both of how good we were together. After plenty of talking and some quality fake tear sound effects, I had fixed what I had broken. And for those of you who say, "It wouldn't be me." That's bullshit. Talking slick and slinging dick will always save you. Always. Two more stupid bitches.

SUNDAY

"RING... RING... RING."

It's 1:55 in the morning on a Sunday and my phone is ringing. I guess Joe was right; a true playa never gets a chance to sleep. Maybe if I ignore it, whoever it is will get the message and hang up.

"RING... RING... RING."

I guess not. "Hello," I said with sleep still in my voice.

"I want you right now."

"What?"

"I want you right now," the voice repeated.

"Who the hell is this?" That didn't go over well with the soft voice on the other end of the phone.

"Oh, so now you don't know who it is?"

Now I was starting to get irritated. "If I knew who the hell it was, I wouldn't be asking."

"It's me, Shawn."

As soon as I heard the name, her face and everything else popped up in my head as if she were standing right there. I cleared the sleep from my throat and said, "Could you repeat what you just said?"

"I want you right now, come and get me." She repeated in a sexy voice.

I thought about it for ten seconds. "Are you ready now?

"Right now." She replied with a tone that was becoming more sexually aggressive with every word.

"Ok, I'm on my way."

I jumped out of bed, grabbed a pair of jeans, threw on some sneakers and was in the car in record time. Shawn didn't live that far from me, so it only took about ten minutes of reckless driving to get to her house. I bailed out of the car and ran up to her door. The way that she had called and demanded that I come get her had, a brother kind of amped. I rang the intercom outside of her building. She lived in a six family house so I had to guess which bell had the last name that I thought would fit with her first name. I've been here before, but I really don't get into last names and all that stuff.

"I'll be right out," came from the speaker on the wall. Good guess. The front door to the building had windows, so I could see her when she came out of her apartment. I heard her apartment door open and then she appeared around the corner of the hallway. Shawn is a specimen of a woman. She's brown skin, 5'10" with a small waist. Her shoulder length hair fit her face perfectly. She had on a pair of ass hugging Capri pants and a tank top. She opened the door and gave me a hug and sensual kiss, just like she always did. I met Shawn around Christmas time a couple of years ago. We dated for a while, but it was obvious that we were going to become fuck buddies. Besides, Shawn has a male attitude about sex and relationships so I couldn't trust her any more than she could trust me.

"What's up baby?" A night of partying was on her breath.

"Nothing, just chillin."

As soon as we got into the car she leaned over and unzipped my jeans.

"Can't you wait?"

"Nope, do I have to?"

"No, not at all." As I started the car, she began to massage between my legs, which made me swell up instantly. I put the car into reverse, backed up and zoomed out of the parking lot. As soon as I got into the street, she went down and took me into her mouth. Her mouth was hot like chicken grease. I wanted to lay back and close my eyes so bad that I started to pull over and park.

"Hurry up and get to your house," came from between my legs.

When I arrived at my house, I screeched into a parking space like the FBI was chasing me. We got out of the car and hurried toward the house. Her ass was looking so tasty in those Capri pants as she walked in front of me. We got inside of the house and went straight to my bedroom.

"You ready?" she said.

"I'm always ready."

She gave me a devilish grin and began to get right up in my face. She pulled me close to her and kissed me with more passion than she ever did before. She was acting like an animal, maybe because we only got together every once and awhile. She stripped me down and shoved me back onto my bed. She ran her tongue all over me. She sucked my fingers and my toes. No bullshit. She stood over me and undressed herself seductively. After she took all of her clothes off, she turned me over onto my stomach and began to run her hot mouth down my back. Her nails dug into my back as she went lower down my torso. It was hot and sweat dripped from my nose from all the friction that our bodies generated from grinding together. I tried to roll over onto my back, but she would not let me. All of a sudden she slowed her pace and began to kiss me gently down the middle of my back. She went down around my lower back straight to my ass. She stroked the back of my legs with her warm soft hands. Gently she parted my cheeks and slid her tongue into the crease of my ass. "OH MY GOD." I let out a moan that sounded as if I was turning into a werewolf. I guess she learned some new tricks since the last time I saw her. She used her tongue to massage any areas that could be reached. By the time she finished, I was about to explode. I had so much tension built up that I knew that when I came, it would be a good one. Shawn and I were very sexually compatible from day one. We didn't get together often but when we did it was something special. She decided that it was time for her to get what she came for. She rolled me onto my back and just watched as my dick stood at attention. She stood up and went over to my nightstand and retrieved a condom. Repetition made her know where I kept them. She took the black condom, better known as "Midnight Desire," my favorite, out of its unusual looking black wrapping and slowly placed it on the head of my shaft, rolling it all the way down to the base. When she mounted me, the warmth of her thighs engulfed me. She started slowly and then began to pick up her pace. As she found her rhythm she started to glisten with sweat. She moved with a purpose. I laid back and watched as I could see the orgasm building up on her face. I always try to pay attention to these things because you always get brownie points for coming at the same time that they do. Soon she was at a feverish pitch, bucking like a wild bronco.

"I'm about to cum," she gasped.

Faster and faster she went until finally she let out her patented, "Oh Isaac." And at the same time I blasted into the condom. We lay in our own sweat panting trying to catch our breath, which gave me time to reflect on what had just happened. What she did, although good, had me wondering about who else she had done it to. Shawn for the most part was a female me. And from that thought alone, I knew it was time for her to get up and go, and not come back. Oh well. Shit happens.

MONDAY

The bass from the speakers thundered like a tropical storm. The DJ's music selections were in perfect timing with the surroundings. The sounds of the Witch Doctor blared through the air, intertwining with the sexual tension that saturated the walls of confined party space. This was just one of many typical Monday nights at the World of Paradise. The World of Paradise is a small Go-Go bar that doubles as a party spot on Monday nights. The atmosphere is very much different than most clubs that you might go to. Because at the World of Paradise. All the freaks come out, especially on Monday nights. The stage is packed with a constant stream of male and female dancers gyrating their bodies together. The diverse crowd consisted of gay men, gay women, bi, tri, or whatever other sexual combination you can imagine, and the DJ is by far the best in the area.

I was with Mekhi and Sun. These are the two guys that I hang out with regularly. They are my best friends. Mekhi is of South African decent and it shows in his high cheekbones and slanted eyes. His sense of style definitely fits his slender, 6'2" frame. He has a smooth way about him that causes women to gravitate to his ethnic aura.

Sun on the other hand is a little shorter, maybe about 5'11" and always has on some tight ass shirt, trying to show off his "I go to the gym" body. Sun's government name is Henry Wynn, but he is on some five-percenter shit these days, thus the name Sun.

We had been at the World of Paradise for about an hour, looking to see what fish could be caught for a late night trick. Mekhi leaned over to me to cut down on having to yell over the music.

"These bitches are here strictly on some looking to get fucked shit," he said in my left ear.

I agreed. "No doubt, why else would they come to a place that has male and female strippers on stage getting their freak on."

"I know that's what I'm here for." Sun chimed in. "Yeah we should pick something up here easy."

"Can I help you?" the bartender butted in.

"Yeah, let me get a Red Devil, a peach martini, and a Corona with lime." We had all been hanging out and partying for so long that I knew their first choice of drinks like the back of my hand.

"Yo, I gotta take a leak, I'll be right back." I made my way through the crowded little bar to the back where the bathrooms were. By the time I came back to the bar, Mekhi had that look of success on his face. Then I noticed two PYTs standing in between Sun and him. As I approached, he turned to face the girls and tapped them on their shoulders.

"This is my man Isaac, the third musketeer."

"What's up ladies? Y'all here giving your money to the stripper men?" They both laughed at my little comment, the one closer to me put out her hand and said, "Hi, I'm Sheila." She was light skinned with long brown hair that was pulled back in a ponytail. She had on a beige leather jean jacket, tight jeans and a tube top. Her body type was slender, just the way we like them. The other girl introduced herself as Simone. She looked pretty much like Sheila with the only difference being Simone having freckles.

Mekhi pulled me close to him.

"We can definitely do a thing with these two."

A thing was the code word that we used for an orgy.

"That's cool with me."

The four of them sat and chitchatted while I watched the dancers. About ten minutes later, I got the nod from Sun. That meant that they were with whatever.

"We're about to get outta here," Mekhi said. "We're going to the house."

The martinis that he had were taking affect on his already chinky eyes. Mekhi and Sun were roommates who had an apartment on the other side of Newark by Georgia King Village.

"I'm gonna finish my drink and I'll be right behind you." I gulped down my drink and headed out. As I came outside the cool breeze of the night air hit my face. The air wasn't as chilly as it was the night of the Lisa/Sada caper, as it had become affectionately known between the three of us. I jumped in the car and started down Union Avenue to Springfield Avenue. There were a lot of people out, which was unusual for a Monday night. As I went down Springfield Ave., I decided to go across Irvine Turner Blvd. I made a left and went straight across. Jammin' 105.1 was playing Al Green as I cruised along in a bit of a daze. I stopped at the corner of Irvine Turner and South Orange Ave. I noticed a car coming up along side of me. Being nosey, I glanced over to see who was in the car. There were two women, both about forty. Both looked like they had been out partying all night, both looked giddy. "Easy pickings," I thought to myself. I gave them a quick smile and turned to face forward. Then, I heard the horn blow. As I looked over, the passenger was rolling down her window.

"How are you?" She asked.

"Fine," I replied, acting as if I really did not want to be bothered.

"Where are you going?"

I did my best puppy dog face as I replied. "Just going to check out a couple friends."

"At this hour?" The passenger replied.

"Yep, feeling a little bored, I guess I'll hang with them for awhile."

She made a concerned facial expression, "I'm kind of bored too!"

"Really," I said in a low deep voice. "Why don't you get your friend to pullover and we can talk about it."

She paused for a moment to collect her thoughts. Whatever she had been drinking had slowed her reaction time. I could see that her friend was become a bit impatient. We had been sitting at the light for a while, but it was 2:30 in the morning and there was no traffic coming or going. Then she answered.

"I live about three blocks from here, follow us and we can talk on my porch."

"Ok, cool."

They pulled off in front of me. We went about two blocks, made a right and then pulled over in front of Society Hill. Society Hill is a city within the city. From the outside, they kind of resemble the brownstones that you would see in Brooklyn. This was where the peoples who had a little more money lived. I got out of the car first. As she got out of the car, I could hear her friend saying, "If you don't call, I'm calling the police." Is this Bitch serious? I know that I don't look like any of the desperate cats that she probably deals with. When she got out of the car, I finally had a chance to see what I was working with. She was about 5'5" with cocoa brown skin and auburn hair done in that Anita Baker hairstyle. Her body was stacked, big ol' titties, big ol' legs, she will do.

"Allow me to introduce myself properly. My name is Isaac' Jordan." I said as her friend drove away.

"Hello, Isaac' Jordan, my name is Kamila Jackson, nice to meet you."

She turned and waved giving me the "follow me" gesture. As we walked up her walkway, I noticed how well manicured the lawn was and how clean the whole area was in general. It was a bit foreign to me. Where I lived, it was clean, but nothing like this. She went up the stairs and sat down on the top step. I didn't want to crowd her space too much, so I sat a couple of stairs below her. We sat talked about where she had been, where I had been.

"Damn I have to use the little girl's room," she said.

"Well go ahead, I'll be right here."

"You can come if you want."

Without hesitation, I stood up and followed.

"Excuse the mess, my son doesn't like to clean up."

"Son?"

"Yes, son."

"How old is he?"

"Twenty."

"Great," I thought, he's going to come home at two something in the morning, see me here, and not be amused. Fuck him, I'm here for one thing, and one thing only. Her apartment had a lived in feeling to it. It wasn't messy, but it wasn't neat either. And her furniture had an antique look about it. When she went to the bathroom, I decided to look around. I browsed at the pictures on her end tables. There was a picture of this big ass young guy. That had to be her son. There were pictures of all these other guys, brothers maybe. As I got closer to the table at the end of the couch, I noticed that the draw was open. Sitting right inside was a wad of money with a rubberband around it. When I heard the toilet flush, I scurried like the rat bastard that I am, back to the other side of the living room and sat down. When she came out, she looked a bit fresher than before.

"Would you like something to drink?"

"Sure, what do you have?"

As I followed her to the kitchen I was watching her ass switch back and forth.

"I got Pepsi."

"Works for me."

I took the glass, went back into the living room and sat down.

"Who are all these guys in this picture?"

That's when the bullshit started.

"My brothers, they are all cops, so that means if you try anything they'll come after you,"

I laughed as if I was amused even though I wasn't. At that moment, I wished that I would not have asked. She started talking and talking and talking. Dropping names like I supposed to be impressed. She beat me in the head about every person that she met or knew. The way she was talking, I could tell that she was spewing nothing but lies. I guess the alcohol had her stories all jumbled together. She talked so much that I wanted to scream. Then all of a sudden she got up and went over to the drawer with the money in it. I think that she noticed it while her head was spinning around talking all that bullshit. She went over and took the money.

"Why does he keep leaving my stash money out like this, I told him not to keep doing this, someone could just walk by and take it."

Exactly what I was thinking. She took the money out of my sight and came back a couple minutes later. I glanced over at the small digital clock on her table. It read 3:27. She had been talking so much that I didn't even realize how long I had been sitting there.

"It's getting late and I have to get up early tomorrow, I'd better go."

"Ok."

Her tone was somber, as if she didn't want me to go.

"Don't look so sad, we'll hook up again," I said as I put my arms out to give her a hug.

We pressed up against each other a little harder than I expected. Her breasts were firm and her nipples were erect. As we hugged I started to run my hands down her back to her ass. She didn't stop me, so I decided to go a little further. I ran my tongue down the side of her neck. She let out purr as if she were a big kitten. That meant that it was on.

I broke away from her and took her by the hand and led her to the stairs. She took the lead and went up the stairs to her bedroom. Once we got into her bedroom, I figured that I better get this thing started before she changed her mind. When we kissed it was hard and wild. The smell of the Hennessy that she had been drinking engulfed my head and went up my nose. "Yuck!" I thought. That Hennessy shit makes me sick to my stomach. She unbuttoned my pants and slid her warm hands down the back of my boxers. She squeezed my ass tightly with both hands. Then she ran her hands around to the front using her left hand to caress my manliness. Her hands felt good against my flesh. As I dug my nails deep into her back, she arched her back and stood up on her toes. I raised her skirt and moved her panties to the side, her pussy was sopping wet. The alcohol and the entire situation really seemed to turn her on. She pushed me back on the king-sized bed and pulled up my shirt. She ran her tongue up and down my stomach, unbuttoning my pants at the same time. Her actions let me know that she was very anxious. She pulled my boxers down in the front, just enough to release me. She took me inside of her mouth, which was a pleasant surprise. Generally, women don't give head as soon as they meet you. Her mouth was warm and extra moist, so moist that when I looked down I could see the saliva from her mouth running down her hand. Her age began to show as she moved her mouth up and down my shaft. Young girls play games with the dick. She seemed to be enjoying it more than me, but then again, a little overacting can get you far. I moaned and squirmed as if she was giving the best head I ever had. The more I moved the more she went wild.

"Do you like the way it feels?" She asked with some insecurity.

I nodded yes and reached into my pocket for a condom. We always took condoms to the World of Paradise, always. When I took my hand out of my pocket, she grabbed my wrist.

"You don't have to."

"What?"

"You don't have to put one on."

"Yes I do."

Her statement made me realize how stupid she really was. She just met me and wanted me to go raw! I strapped up and took my pants off. I pulled her skirt up and reached down to take her panties off. They were already gone, great job. I slid myself inside of her, she was soaking wet. She made noises as if she had not been fucked in a decade. I rolled her over on her back and began to use my 6'1", 200 pound frame to take full advantage of her. She moved as if she never had sex with anyone with an imagination before. I did my best to turn her body inside out. After I was done I laid there for awhile thinking. Thinking about other women, thinking about some things that I had to do. Most of all, thinking about the excuse I was going to give her so that I could leave. She didn't know anything about me so I could tell her anything.

"Hey," I whispered. "Wake up, I have to go."

The clock next to the bed flashed 5:21.

"I have to be at work at ten."

"You can stay here and leave later, I'll make you breakfast." She said.

"I have to shower and change for work. And since I don't have any clothes here, that is not an option. So I had better go home."

She nodded to say that she understood. I got up to put my clothes on and then headed for the door.

"Wait!" She said at the last minute as she jumped up and grabbed a bathrobe hanging on her closet door. She went over to her dresser and took a pen and started writing on a post-it. She followed me down the stairs to the front door, the whole time writing on the paper. When I opened the door she said. "Here, take my number." I took the paper and looked down to read it. On it was her job number, her home number, her cell number and her beeper number. I had obviously done a great job.

"Call me tomorrow from work so we can talk, and you can tell me what it is that you do, that has you leaving me at 5 in the morning," She said.

"Ok, I'll do that."

I walked down about four stairs stopped and turned around. Kamila was standing there watching me; she had that look on her face as if she knew that she would never see me again. You know the kind of look you get when you park your car in a bad neighborhood. As soon as she closed the door, I dropped the paper right in her walkway. I wonder if she found it the next day when she came out. Dumb bitch. You would think a woman that old wouldn't be so stupid.

TUESDAY

I'm so glad that I don't have the conventional 9 to 5 job because if I did, I would probably be unemployed. I sell artwork at The City Without Walls Art Gallery in downtown Newark. All the late night partying I do is definitely not for someone who has to get up early. It's about 10 o'clock so I guess I'll get myself some breakfast and go in about twelve. I light two vanilla scented candles, put Michelle N'degecello in the CD player and jump in the shower. When I get out of the shower, I put some Right Guard on and splash on some Ck One to get the right smell.

"Let's see, I guess I'll keep it simple today. Jeans, Paisley button up shirt, and of course, shell toe Adidas."

When I finally get outside, it is a beautiful sunny day. Not too hot, about seventy-five degrees with a light breeze. I cruise into downtown Newark about 11:30. The area is buzzing with people everywhere. The ladies are out extra strong today. As I come to the light at Broad and Market Streets, I put in Maxwell's *Now* CD and turn up the volume. The young girls walking across the street start dancing to the heavy bass line of "Lifetime." The young girls these days must be on steroids because they are all built as if they were in their mid-twenties. It takes a lot of restraint these days as a man whore to not mess with any of these supple young girls. Always remember. 15 will get you 20. You know 15 years in age will get you 20 years in jail. It takes me about five minutes to arrive at the parking lot behind Penn Station.

As I step out of the car, I notice out of the corner of my eye, a young lady in the distance coming towards me. As she moves closer I stand motionless. She is my prototype dream woman and I do mean WOMAN. She was about 5'8", definitely a size 6. She was light skinned, not in yellow kind of a way. But something better, smoother. More like buttermilk. She had a close-cut natural crop with the kind of hair that gets curly when it is wet. She wore no make-up, just clear lip gloss and none of that fake nail tips bullshit either. Just natural. "Wow," I said to myself. I have got to make a move or I'll be mad for the rest of the day. I started towards her with my usual swagger, but as I got right in front of her, something about her movement made me suddenly cautious. And she knew it. I messed around and let her walk right past me.

"Get, yourself together you pussy," I thought to myself. I whirled around.

"Excuse me,"

But she made no reply and kept walking.

"Excuse me," I said louder.

Still, no reply. I know she heard me because the first time I said something she paused and slowed down before moving again. "Fuck this. I'm going to get her." I jogged up behind her as calmly as I could. As soon as I got behind her she turned around.

"I heard you calling me. I just wanted to see if you would chase me."

I was totally stunned by that statement. I'm really not accustomed to chasing a woman.

"My name is Sakeena, What's yours?"

When she spoke I was in a complete daze. "What the hell is going on?" I asked myself. I was nervous as hell.

"What, you're not going to answer me now?"

That snapped me out of my trance.

"Uh...yeah, I mean yes. My name is Isaac'" I said, my voice fluttering the way it did when I had a crush on my second grade teacher.

As I spoke I looked down at the ground. Why did I do that? This woman had the prettiest feet that I had ever seen. Straight up, no bullshit. That was it. I think I just found Mrs. Jordan.

"I was just wondering where you were going?" I said nervously.

"You can do better than that can't you Isaac', can't you?" she replied. "Are you trying to tell me that you watched me come down the street and then chased me down just to ask me where I was going?"

Now she was fucking with me. I like that. Fine as hell and she ain't no idiot. Before I could say anything she said, "I have to get moving, but if you can think of something better. Call me." She reached into her purse pulled out a small black organizer and gave me a card. "Don't forget, something better," she said as turned around and walked away. "What just happened?" I asked myself. "Did she just pimp me?" I stood there for a second just blinking my eyes as if someone had just slapped me in my face. I looked down at the card. It simply said, Sakeena Thomas/Angel on Earth/ (973) 555-1202.

As I walked through Penn Station, I was still in a bit of a stupor. Ms. Thomas left quite an impression that I could not shake, which was a new feeling for me. Under normal circumstances I was always cool around women, but a few minutes ago I found myself completely out-classed in the game of first meetings. All I could think about for the rest of the day was Sakeena. Her brashness, her look, even her fragrance still lingered in my head. I couldn't wait to tell somebody about her. As soon as I got home, I called Sun. Sun answered the phone on the first ring.

"Yo, I was just about to call you," he screamed into the phone.

"Let me tell you about this female that I met today," I said.

But before I could say another word, he cut me off.

"Later for that, I got something better," he yelled.

He only gets excited like this when he thinks he has something good for us to get into.

"Just tell me that you're not doing anything?" he asked.

"No I'm not doing anything important. But I can tell by the excitement in your voice, I take it that I, or we, will be." I replied.

"Listen, I got Sheila over here at the house. I got the drinks, I got the music and I got the porno. All I need now is you."

"First of all, who the hell is Sheila and where is she while you are talking like this about the Thing."

He paused for a second.

"She's in the bathroom. Remember those two chicks from World P.? She's one of them and I know that she's with the threesome. Here she comes, come through."

And he hung up.

"Do I really need to go over there and get into this," I thought. "Hell yes!" I hopped in the car and was there in no time. I could hear the music vibrating against the door. When Sun came to the door, he was already down to jeans and no shirt.

"What's up playa?" he said shaking my hand.

"You know. Same soup, just reheated."

As I followed him, the smell of incense was hovering in the air. I walked into the living room and there she was, Sheila. She was sitting on the futon looking at TV. I had to shake my head when I realized what she was watching. Big Black Cocks Volume 14,

37

Sun's favorite porno video.

"How are you?" She said.

"I'm chilling."

Apparently, by the look on her face, she remembered me. She was drinking out of a big ass plastic cup.

"What are you drinking?" I asked. Sun stepped in.

"I made her a Long Island Iced Tea."

Again I shook my head. Sun didn't know how to make mixed drinks at all. So it was safe to assume that he had made something that looked like a real drink, but it wasn't. Whatever it was, there was a lot in that cup and it looked like she had already had more than one. I decided to ask about the porno.

"What's up with the movie?"

Sheila looked up at me with a naughty grin on her face. "I like pornos, is that bad?"

"No not at all."

Sun made the let's make a move gesture, while Sheila watched Julian St. Jock and Jake Steed punish this girl on the screen. Sun sat down next to her and started talking.

"You ever thought about doing something like that?" he asked.

"No," she giggled.

Now I knew that this girl was stupid. I went over to the stereo and took out one of Sun's rump shaker CD's. I put it in and pushed play. When the music came on, I turned the volume up to eight. Since I am bolder than the others, I turned to Sheila and said. "How about you dance for us?"

At first she just looked at me as if she didn't understand.

"I'm tippin."

Dumb bitch took the bait. She stood up and started to move to the music of Luke. She started to get into it more when I walked up to her and stuck a couple of singles into her jeans. Sun followed my lead and stood up behind her. We started to move our bodies together as one. I looked over her shoulder at Sun. "Now," I mouthed to him.

I leaned in and kissed her right in her mouth. No resistance, which was a good sign. Sun reached around her and started to rub her breast. At the same time, I used my right hand to unbutton her jeans and my left to unsnap her bra. I knelt down in front of her and pulled her jeans down; she stepped right out of them. Very Good. She extended her arms to make space between the three of us and pulled her shirt over her head. She looked good standing there in her panties. I lay back on the couch and pulled her down on top of me. Sun stripped down to nothing fast as hell. She unbuckled my belt and unzipped my pants. She immediately took me into her mouth. Sun went and turned the lights off. He walked over to the window and slightly opened the blinds, allowing the moonlight to shine through. I could still see his silhouette moving around in the dimly lit room. Then he came up behind her and took her panties off. I guess he was fumbling with a condom, because one went flying over her back and landed on my chest. When he entered her, she let out the classic porno moan. Looks like Vol.14 had an influence. Sun started fucking her hard as hell from the back. I had to give him the calm down face because she was about to cut my dick to pieces with her teeth. I had to get up before this guy caused me some bodily harm. I sat up and slid myself from under her. I stood up next to the couch and undressed. That's when this episode started to get serious.

"Yo kid, lay down," Sun said.

After he made Sheila stand up, I laid down on my back on the futon. He took one of the condoms on the end table and gave it to her. This is when I started to wonder if she was telling the truth about her not having done this before. She took the condom out of the wrapper with her hands and put it in her mouth. Then she took me in her mouth again, rolling the condom down with her mouth. I'm impressed. Then Sun instructed Sheila to mount me. As she begins to ride me, this nigga Sun gets on the futon behind her and tries to fuck her in the ass. As soon as he got his dick half way in her, she let out one hellafied yell. But I will say one thing; she took that shit like a champ. Everything was going well until Sun started trying to really bust her ass. She violently bucked him off of her. Sun was in rare form tonight. He got off of the futon and walked around the table in front of the futon. Then he tries to stand up over me and put his beef in Sheila's mouth. Sounds good, except that's a little too close for my comfort.

"I think we had better go for something more conventional," I said.

I told her to get up and lay on her back. When she lay down, Sun jumped right on top of her. He put her legs up on his shoulders and started dogging her out. This chick was really on some other shit. She reached out and pulled me towards her and put me right in her mouth. Her fellatio was incredible. I came in her mouth in about 10 minutes. Then I decided to get involved in Sun's exploits. I grabbed Sheila by her ankles and pulled her legs as far apart as I could. She let out all kinds of noises then. I could hear how wet her pussy had gotten. She started screaming as Sun pounded away at her. Then her Jones came down. She dug her nails deep into Sun's back. I had to let go of her legs because she started to kick and squirm all over the place. Sun laid on top of her for a couple of minutes. When he stood up, we gave each other the sneaky high five.

"That was pretty cool," he said.

"Ya think?"

Now that it was over, I looked down at Sheila lying on the futon and she looked exhausted.

"I gotta get outta here," I said to Sun as I pulled my pants up. He gave me that "Don't just leave me with her" look. But before he could say anything I was heading out the door.

"It was definitely a pleasure seeing you again," I said as I went out.

"Where do we find the stupid ass ho bitches?" I asked myself as I started back home. "What difference does it make anyway? The more stupid the better. Another one bites the dust."

WEDNESDAY

After last night's activity with Sun, I still went to sleep thinking about Sakeena. I'm still not sure what it was about her that made me nervous when I approached her. I'm not the type to be stuttering and acting like a school boy because of a woman. Now that I made myself look like an idiot when I spoke to her, I had to figure out how I could recover from that moment of weakness. I picked up the card she gave me off of my nightstand. Her fragrance was still on it. "It makes no sense to be scared now, I might as well call and see what happens," I said to myself. "Here we go."

I began to dial the number on the card. The more numbers I dialed, the more nervous I became. One more number to go, I hang up. As soon as I hang up the phone it rings.

"What's up Mr. Jordan?" Mekhi's voice bellows over the phone.

"Nothing man. I was about to call this fine ass sister that I met yesterday, but I sold out and hung up?"

"Hung up, for what? Being scared of a bitch ain't your thing," he replied sarcastically.

That statement pissed me off a little bit. Although I had only been with her for five minutes, I could just feel that she didn't fall into the "Bitch" category.

"First of all, she's not a bitch. Second of all, I'm not scared. Now you're not respecting me. On top of that, I probably would have called her if you wouldn't have called me and broke my concentration."

"Yeah, whatever. Later for that, I'm going to work from my laptop today. So what's up with lunch in Soho?" he asked.

"I'm with that. I just have to stop by the gallery, make a sale, and we're out."

I took a quick shower, put on some smell goods and looked in the closet for something to wear. "I think I'll dress way down today. Cargo pants, wife beater and most definitely, shell toe Adidas." As soon as I got dressed I called Mekhi and told him to meet me at Penn Station. I grabbed my backpack and got myself a cab.

When I got inside the station, Mekhi was already waiting in front of Blimpie's, our usual meet up spot. As usual, Mekhi looked like he was posing to be an Ebony male model. He had on some beige linen pants and long sleeved white button up. When I got close to him I couldn't help but notice his feet.

"You are the man," I said as we shook hands. He gave me that I don't know, but I do know look.

"What?" he said with a smirk.

"What? Don't act like you don't know. What's up with the mules?" This guy had on some brown leather mules.

"Those are hot, what are they?" I asked.

"Kenny Cole, you know how I do."

Before we went up to the platform, we stopped and got a couple of beers. As we headed towards the escalator, I saw this Amazon type female coming towards us.

"Check that out," I said as I motioned towards the young lady coming towards us.

"Damn," Mekhi replied as if he had never seen anything like her before.

She was about 5'10" with honey brown skin. Her hair was long and straight, pulled back into a ponytail. She was obviously looking for attention with her choice for the day's wear. She had on a denim mini-skirt and a tight fitting long sleeved blouse. The kick ass was that she only had one button in the middle fastened. Her legs were long, and muscular, with a tattoo that started under the skirt and ended mid thigh. She had another tattoo across her cleavage that she wasn't trying to hide. As she walked by, we both just stood and gazed at her like two kids in a candy store. I didn't say anything because I thought that Mekhi was. That's probably why he didn't say anything either.

When we got on the train, it was being held in the station for a couple minutes waiting to get as many people on as possible. Just as the door was about to close, The Amazonian came running into our car. She was panting like a dog trapped in a car during the summer. As the train started to move, I noticed that she was using one hand to hold onto the pole and the other to hold her shirt. The beginning of the train ride was quiet until I noticed that the Amazon girl was laughing to herself. At first, I thought she had thought of something funny, but she kept on doing it. After a couple of minutes, Mekhi noticed and began to look at me. We've been friends long enough to talk without talking, so I knew exactly what he was thinking. She looked over at him and chuckled.

"What?" He said.

"Nothing." Her voice was as smooth as her long muscular legs.

She giggled again. Mekhi's aggressive nature seemed to overcome him in seconds.

"What are you laughing at?" he asked, moving closer to her.

"Nothing," she said again.

I saw the frustration come over his face. When he got irritated, his accent became heavy.

"Then why the fuck do you keep laughing?"

That seemed to interest her.

"Come over here and I'll tell you," she said as she motioned to him.

When he moved, I moved. We both walked over to her side of the train. Mekhi leaned close to her and said, "Now, tell me what's so funny." All of a sudden, she jerked and folded her arms. It happened so fast that I didn't even see why she did it.

"Sorry if I scared you."

"No problem, Now tell us what's so funny."

She looked around the train. "Well sometimes when I'm on the train, or around a lot of people, I imagine them in there underwear. It makes the time on the train pass by fast."

I had to interrupt. "Did you do that with us?" I asked.

"No I didn't get to you yet."

The tone that she used was kind of ditsy, so I knew that she wasn't too bright. I glanced over at Mekhi and did that eye contact communicating shit. He knew that with the right line of bullshit, this chick was definitely a threesome candidate.

"So what are you going to the city for?" Mekhi asked.

"Just chillin, I like to walk around and look at all the different things."

"Why don't you come with us?"

"I don't even know y'all."

"So what?"

Mekhi's tone was rude and abrasive. I could tell that her airhead persona was quickly beginning to aggravate him. I leaned over to her and said, "Look, we're going to be in New York City in broad daylight. What could we possibly do to you that you don't want done. Besides, I would enjoy your company." By the look on her face, I was just waiting for the "Ok I'll come" answer. And sure enough, it came.

"Alright I'll tag along with you and your friend, but no funny stuff."

"Of course not." Mekhi muttered.

Once we arrived in New York, we decided to go get something to eat. We went to Bar Six on Sixth Avenue. It's one of those nice little cafes with tables in front so you can sit outside. Mekhi likes to get his drink on, so he ordered a martini, his usual. I wasn't in a drinking mood so I ordered a Pepsi with a slice of lemon.

"You know what?" Mekhi chimed in.

"We haven't had a formal introduction. My name is Mekhi and this is my man Isaac'. And you are?" He said as he extended his hand.

"Natalie. That's who I am. Y'all don't mind if I call you Batman and Robin instead, because it doesn't seem like you two don't do much without each other."

The way that she said that made me give Mekhi that threesome look again. After a couple of drinks, Natalie started to loosen up more than she already was. She started touching and feeling the both of us while laughing and giggling. A woman that acts like an idiot can be nerve racking, but to get what I want, I'll tolerate it. All I had to do was keep Mekhi from getting too aggravated and we were in there. While she was laughing and acting stupid, I noticed that she had a tongue ring. I looked over to Mekhi and gave him the "I'll take it from here" look.

"So," I said. "What's up with the tongue ring? What do you use it for?"

"I just wanted it," she replied.

"That's a bunch of bullshit, everyone who has one has it for one reason or another. Most people use it for pleasuring either a he or a she." I could tell that she admired my forwardness. Now it was time to see where she was at.

"I've never kissed anyone with a pierced tongue before," which was entirely true.

"Oh really?" So are you asking me for a kiss even when I haven't known you for more than an hour?"

"Well if you do kiss me, maybe you will get to know me better." Not even two minutes later, we were tongue kissing like we had been in a relationship for years. As we kissed, I would glance over her shoulder at Mekhi to see the thoughts in his eyes. And I could tell that it was time to make a move towards Jersey to his place. When I pulled away from Natalie she had that hot and horny look.

"Na-Na, why don't you come back to my house with me and I'll make you a home cooked dinner. Then we can kick back and chill. Oh, by the way you don't mind if I call you Na-Na do you?"

"Ok No,"

"Ok, No, what does that mean?"

"Ok, I'll come to your place. And no, I don't mind if you call me Na-Na."

"Cool then let's go."

On the way back to Jersey, I kept the kissing and cuddling going in order to keep the fish marinating. Mekhi played the uninterested role very well so that she wouldn't suspect anything. We arrived at Penn Station and got a cab to Mekhi's house. When we got to his house, I said, "We're gonna go inside and get a bottle of wine from Mekhi's stash, then go to my house."

As we entered Mekhi and Suns apartment, Mekhi's heritage was everywhere. He has all different kinds of African figurines throughout the living room. I've been here plenty of times, but Na-Na meandered around as if she was in a museum.

"I'll be right back, I'm going to get a bottle of wine and then we can go. Please feel free to make yourself at home." I said motioning towards the couch. I didn't realize how literally she would take that statement as I followed Mekhi upstairs to his bedroom.

As soon as he closed the door to his bedroom he said, "I know we can fuck this silly bitch."

"There's no doubt about that," I said as I retrieved a bottle from his personal stash. "I'll start her drinking. We should be bustin' her ass in about twenty or thirty minutes." I grabbed a couple of glasses and headed back to the living room.

When I got back to the living room, I was surprised to see that Natalie had taken her shoes off and was lounging on the couch. She saw the two glasses.

"I thought we were taking the bottle and leaving?" she said.

"Well, it looks to me as if you've made yourself at home. So I really don't think it makes a difference now anyway." I sat next to her and handed her a glass.

"Here's to new friends." The way that she sucked the wine down I thought that she knew what Mekhi and I had in mind.

"Damn! Are you thirsty or something?" I stated sarcastically. How about I go and get Bilal's CD and we just stay here for a while?" She reached out and took my glass from me.

"I think that I can work with that," she said as she started to drink from my glass.

I stood up and turned around on some cool smooth shit like Billy Dee in *Lady Sings the Blues* and walked away. As soon as I got out of her sight, I raced up the stairs and busted into Mekhi's bedroom. He was lying back on the bed sipping on a glass of wine.

"Yo! Gimmie a hat and come downstairs in twenty minutes."

He reached over to his nightstand and handed me a condom and sent me on my way. I went back to the living room with CD in hand and condom in my pocket ready to go. By the time I returned, she had finished with the glass of wine and was sprawled out on the couch. I guess because she was drinking the wine so fast, it had started to kick in. I went over and sat down next to her.

"So," I asked.

"You're sure it's ok that we stay here?" She asked while nodding her head yes.

I was absolutely positive that the wine had taken effect. "Would you like some more wine?"

"No, no thank you. I feel a little warm as it is."

That was my cue. I moved in a little closer to her. Her eyes were glazed like a Christmas ham.

"Do you think I could get some of that pierced tongue thing again?" I asked as I inched closer to her.

"I don't see why not," she mumbled as our lips met.

As soon as I touched her, she let out a moan. At the same time, that little ass shirt she was wearing popped open. I ain't gonna lie; she had some pretty ass tits. I lowered my head and began to run my tongue between her supple breasts. The harder I sucked on her nipples the more she tugged and pulled at my pants. She pushed me away from her and said, "Lye back." So of course, I did. She undid my pants and I lifted my ass so she could pull them down to my ankles. She started using the tip of her tongue to trace an imaginary figure eight around my shaft and sack. Good money! Na-Na definitely knew how to use her tongue piercing. She ran her tongue up and down my flagpole. The best thing of all, she had an incredibly, wet sloppy mouth. Remember, the wetter the better ladies. I laid back and closed my eyes as she went to work. Then all of a sudden she stopped. I opened my eyes to see why she would stop giving me some of the best jawbone that I had ever received.

"Y'all two are totally out of control," she said.

I looked up to see Mekhi standing behind her butt ass naked, except for a pair of socks.

"Don't even worry about it. Just keep doin what you doin, and enjoy the experience," Mekhi replied from the now dark room.

51

He started to kiss her down her back as she turned her attention back to my eagerly awaiting manhood. He only kissed her for what seems like about ten seconds. Then he stood up straight and slipped himself into a wetsuit. He entered her about as easily as two guys hitting one girl can possibly get. As time wore on, so did Na-Na's stamina. I could see the wear and tear of two men beginning to come down on her. I really don't like getting head while someone else is fucking anymore, especially after the teeth incident the day before with Sun. So, I removed myself from her mouth, stoop up and watched Mekhi finish his work. As soon as he moved out of the way, I was on her. By now I was ready for this episode to be over. So I went into squirrel mode. Fast and hard was the course that I took. Mekhi kept eye contact with me as I tried my best to punish her just because. He could tell by the look on my face that he would be stuck with her after I was done. As soon as I was through, I pulled out of her. She laid face down on the couch trying to catch her breath. Now this may sound a bit strange, but when I finished, I thought about Sakeena. Mekhi was sitting on the chair across from Na-Na just reflecting on the moment. And so was I. Sometimes dogging women isn't as easy as everyone thinks. That shit wears you out, physically and mentally.

"Yo, I'm going upstairs to make a call," I said as I exited the living room.

By the look on Mekhi's face, he knew who I was going to call. First I had to make a stop in the bathroom and get my shit fresh. I went and sat on Mekhi's bed and picked up the phone. Again when I dialed the number, I felt a little nervous.

"Hello." She said, picking up the phone much quicker than I expected.

"Hello?" She said again.

"Uh, Hi. How are you?"

"I'm Fine. Is this Isaac'?"

Whoa! I'm impressed. She recognized my voice after speaking to me only one time.

"Yes it is. How are you?" I asked again.

"I'm still fine. Are you ok?"

"Yeah, I'm cool. I was just chillin, so I figured that I would call and say hello."

"Well thank you Mr. Jordan. So what's up?"

"Not much. Uhmm, I was thinking that maybe you would like to get together and go out for a drink." Definitely not my style I thought. But it had already come out.

"Ok." she replied quickly.

I wasn't prepared for such a speedy response.

"Look, I'm leaving work early tomorrow, so why don't we meet for lunch? I'll call around 10 tomorrow morning and we'll set something up."

"Sounds good." Before I could say anything else, she said goodbye and hung up.

I went back down to the living room to find Na-Na fully dressed. Mekhi was dressed and sitting in the same spot where I had left him.

"I'm about to get a cab and leave bro," I said to Mekhi as I picked up the phone next to the couch. "I'm sure that you can handle this situation without me."

When the cab came, I expressed my gratitude to Na-Na and made my exit. When I got home, I noticed that I only had two messages on my answering machine. Both from Sada. "Isaac' this is Sada. I just wanted to ask you something, a friend of mine, from school, she said... that you...that she..." She hung up. Her voice was breaking up like she had been or was crying.

"What the fuck was that?" I mumbled to myself.

"Message erased," came from the machine. "Next message."

"Isaac'!" Sada's voice was much more abrupt this time. "Do you think you're some kind of pimp or something? Do you think that you're God's fucking gift to women? Do you think that you're going to be able to run around fucking every woman that you see and not be held accountable for your...?

"Message erased."

Whatever had happened was of no concern of mine. She had probably been talking to one of those bitches at her school that was a psychology major and felt the need to tell her that she knew how guys like me thought. I hate to tell her, but fucking around with a lot of women will make me and every other guy like me better at that physco-babble bullshit then they ever will be. Besides, I can't be worried about that now anyway. I have to get some rest for my lunch with Sakeena tomorrow. Then the phone started ringing. I turn up the volume so that I could hear who it is. "Isaac' I know that you've gotten the other messages! I think...." I just turned the volume down and went on about my business. I'll straighten her out later. Just like Pretty Tony said in *The Mack*. "Once I get a bitch, I got a bitch."

THURSDAY

I'm up early, ready to get in the shower. Today is going to be a good day. I'm waiting for Sakeena to call so we can set up a time to get together. And on top of that, I don't have to go to work. You can't beat that. As I start making my way to the shower the phone starts ringing. It has to be Sakeena. I run over to the phone. "Hello," I say in my low sexy voice.

"Isaac'?"

Wait a minute. That doesn't sound like Sakeena. "Sada?" I question. "Yeah, It's me you son of bitch!" She yells.

"Listen Sada, I don't know what the fuck is wrong with you, but I don't have time for this crazy shit." She didn't reply. "Sada?" "Sada?" Still nothing. "I know one thing, if you don't answer this time you're gonna be hearing the dial tone."

"How could you do this to me?" She finally asked.

"Do what? What are you talking about?" Now my mind is racing because she could be talking about anything or anybody. "I know you're not talking about Lisa. I told you that she didn't mean anything to me." I tried to be as firm as possible. Sada was weak and I knew she would back down. Or at least that's what I thought.

"I went to class the other day and we got a new student. Her name is Shawn. She said that she doesn't live too far from you."

My heart dropped into my stomach. What the hell was Shawn doing at Sada's school? That bitch ain't that bright. "Shawn? Did she say that she knew me?" No need to admit to anything too soon. "Let me think. Do I know anyone named Shawn?" I said aloud. I think that statement sent her over the edge.

"Don't play stupid you fucking asshole. You fucked her! And according to her, you've been fucking her for quite some time. And on top of that, you've been fucking a whole bunch of other bitches too! She told me everything that you told her."

Damn it, this bitch Shawn had turned state's evidence on me. Once we had come to an understanding that we wouldn't be dating exclusively, we would talk about the other people that we would fuck with when we weren't fucking each other. I tried to reply as calmly as I could considering the fact that I was starting to feel like I was about to throw up.

"And your dumb ass believed her. You don't even know her." I said in a condescending tone.

"So what? She knows you, that's for sure. She knows things she could only know if she was fucking you."

Before I could answer, the phone beeped. That was Sakeena for sure. "Hold on."

"No, you piece of shit. I'ma make sure you eat all that pimpin' shit you be talking."

Is she threatening me? "Is that a threat you silly ass bitch?

You damn right I talk that pimpin' shit. You weren't complaining about it when I was wearing your ass out! Now were you?"

"Fuck you!" she screamed before I heard the phone slam in my ear.

Then the phone beeped again. Again. "Shit, Sakeena." I clicked over and tried to catch my breath the best that I could.

"Hello," I gasped.

"Are you busy?" Sakeena's smooth voice came over the phone.

"No, no, no. Not at all. I was on my way to take a shower when I heard the phone ring." She didn't need to know that I was on the phone arguing with that idiot anyway.

"So what's up with today?" she asked.

Just that fast, the smoothness in her voice had settled me down. I think I'm starting to get over the nervousness that is Sakeena. "Whatever you want to do, I'll do. And wherever you want to go, I'll take you. Just as long as I can see you." Saw that in a movie once.

"That sounds very interesting. How about you meet me in the city then?"

I guess she didn't see that movie. "Sounds like a date then. Just tell me the time and the place and I'm there." As soon as she gave me the time and the address I was off of the phone and getting ready with the quickness.

Normally, I was very slow with my movement, but not today. After I got out of the shower I had to figure out what I would wear. I knew that she would be coming from work and would have on some kind of business attire. So I went with something simple that wouldn't make her feel over dressed. I picked a pair of black slacks, a white button up and these banging ass Italian square toed, three quarter lace ups. Now the smell goods. "I think I'll go with the Gautier," I said out loud. I sprayed myself in all my right places. The basic spots. The neck, the wrist, and my own special place, the ankles. "Hey, you never know how freaky some women can be." And just that fast I was out the door and on my way to the city.

Sakeena wanted to meet me at this place called *Charmaine's* on West Broadway in Soho. I found that a little unusual considering that she worked in Midtown. But I guess this place must be good if she was willing to travel this far downtown. As I walked along I tried to imagine what I would do when I saw her. I started whispering lines that I could say like, "Hey baby, how you doin?" Hell no. "What's up Ma?" Most definitely, hell no. Maybe just hello and then I lean in for the kiss on the cheek thing. Maybe. As I turned onto West Broadway, the butterflies started to come again. This is not good. All I have to do is relax and I'll be straight. From where I was, I could see *Charmaine's*, but no Sakeena. Then she suddenly appeared from the doorway. It seemed like everything went into one of those Steve Austin Six Million Dollar man slow motion things.

When she looked my way, a smile came across her face. She looked incredible. She wasn't dressed entirely the way I expected, but still business like. She had on a fitting black skirt that rose just above her knee and a snug red top with spaghetti straps. Her hair was just like before, but on this occasion, it appeared to be more spiked. And of course she had on that clear lip gloss. That drives me bananas. She moved towards me with slow deliberate steps. "Hey you," I said as I took both of her hands and pulled her towards me. Suddenly, I felt at ease. I guess my inner pimp had taken over. When she hugged me, her sweet smell enveloped us. As we pulled apart, she kissed me on the cheek. That was a nice surprise. "So, how are you Ms. Lady?" I asked.

"I'm fine, and you?"

"I'm cool." She turned and motioned for me to follow her. She might have the most perfect shape as far as I can see. She already had a spot for us. *Charmaine's* has a vintage lounge setting. Lots of old furniture, like the kind that your Grandmother had, but without the plastic slipcovers. She had chosen a section that was tucked away in the corner by the window. This section had a couch instead of chairs, with two end tables pushed together in front of it. Even though it was broad daylight outside, the large curtains hanging just below made it seem as if it was evening. We sat down on the couch and started talking about any and everything. She told me that she was a paralegal who wanted to become a lawyer and lived in Montclair. It struck me rather strange that I really didn't mind sitting and talking with her. All that conversation shit is not for me. All I'm ever trying to do is get my fuck on as quick as possible and be out. It was also hard at first for me to except the fact we had so much in common. But after awhile I was just happy that she wasn't an idiot. When we first started talking she was sitting on the other end of the couch. But as the conversation wore on, she started to move closer. She really seemed interested with my hobby of being a painter along with writing poetry and all that other Renaissance Blackman shit.

"So how is it that a man like you doesn't have a woman in his life?"

I knew that was coming. Lucky for me the waiter came before I could reply. After we ordered, the conversation continued. But the interruption broke her train of thought, so the prior question was no longer an issue. She didn't need to know why I haven't had a steady relationship in years. She didn't need to know that I was in love once. Yeah me. As Snoop once said, I was in love like a mutherfucker, licking the pearl tongue. Or as I like to refer to it now, being a sucka for love. Maybe we'll talk about that later. We stayed at *Charmaine's* for about an hour and a half.

"Don't you have to get back to work?" I asked. She looked at me and paused for a second.

"I really don't want to and as a matter of fact I think I won't," she replied as she pulled her cell phone from her purse. She dialed and called her job.

"Hi, this is Keena. I have a few more errands to run, so I probably won't be coming back to the office. If you need me, call me on my cell phone. Thanks."

She was smiling at me the whole time that she was on the phone.

"Well, it looks like you're stuck with me for the rest of the day, if that's ok with you?" She said with a devilish grin on her face.

"That's definitely ok with me." We sat and talked for about ten more minutes. It was amazing to me how much we had in common. It was nice, but at the same time scary. I have grown accustom to not caring about what the women with whom I had encounters with thought of me. So for me, this was refreshing.

"Let's get out of here and go for a walk." I went to the register and paid the check. When we went outside, she took my hand in hers and led the way. That was something else I was not used to. Walking in public holding hands was something I shied away from. You never know who could be watching. But today I said, "Fuck it." We strolled around in Soho window shopping, laughing and joking. It seemed as if I had known her for years. I felt very comfortable with her. And it felt good to finally be with someone who I could talk to that didn't get on my nerves whenever she opened her mouth. When I looked at my watch I was shocked to see how much time had gone by since we first got together. It was almost four thirty.

"I think that we better head back to Jersey. I don't want to get caught in the rush hour crowd." She agreed, so we grabbed a cab back to Penn Station. I liked the train ride home. She cuddled up next to me all the way back to Newark.

"I'm tired. I think that I'm going to go home and take a nap," she said to me as we exited Penn Station.

"All that walking around does have a brother a little tired. How are you going to get home?"

"I'm taking a cab. So I guess that I'll talk to you later?" she said as she flagged down a cab. She moved closer to me and pecked me on the lips. She opened the cab door and got in. I just stood there motionless as the cab drove away. Then the cab suddenly stopped and backed up to where I was standing.

"What's wrong?"

"Nothing," she said in a soft tone. "I was thinking that maybe you…"

"That I would what?" This was the first time that I had seen her unsure of herself.

"That maybe you would come home with me."

I didn't even answer. I opened the door and got in. We held hands the entire time that we were in the cab.

"I hope that you don't mind coming with me. It's just that I haven't met anyone with whom I've had so much in common and enjoyed the time that I spent with them so much," she said.

"Believe me. I completely understand. I feel the same way about being with you," I said as I looked into her big brown eyes.

"Isaac', would I be wrong in saying that I think that you've been hurt before?" Maybe my facial expression indicated that I had been hurt before. I was usually pretty good at hiding it. My lips parted slowly as I answered. "Yes." She leaned into me and kissed me on the lips again. But it wasn't a peck this time.

"I like you a lot already just from being with you today. And I just wanted you to know that I won't..."

"You won't what?"

"I won't hurt you. I know you haven't known me long enough to believe everything that I say. But I thought that I should tell you anyway."

I can't explain why. But at that moment, I knew that all of the shit that I was doing and had done had to come to an end. I couldn't even reply. I just sat there in a daze for the rest of the ride.

We turned down a quiet little street lined with trees. There were a line of two family houses on one side of the street and a park on the other. We exited the cab and walked up the stairs in front of the house. She opened the door to the first floor apartment and gave the follow me look. So of course I did. She gave me a quick tour of her space and then led me to her bedroom. She kicked her shoes off and crawled up onto the queen-sized bed.

"Come," she said as she patted the empty space next to her. "Sit next to me."

Normally I would have been on the bed faster than she could blink. However, this time I waited. I didn't want to seem like I was too thirsty.

"Please," she said with her hand out.

"Ok, but no funny stuff." I replied, moving towards her. She laid down with her back to me. Then she reached around and pulled me close to her softness in the spooning position. I closed my eyes and inhaled her scent. And as crazy as this may sound, we slept. No bullshit! We slept in our clothes, on top of the covers, all night long. Now I know that you were probably thinking that I was going to try and get some ass but I didn't. Fooled you, didn't I?

FRIDAY

As my eyes open I realize that I don't recognize the surroundings I sit up on the bed and try to focus. "Where the hell am I?" Now I remember. I'm at Sakeena's. I must have been really tired yesterday. Sometimes you don't realize how tired your body is until you get a chance to sleep. I look over at the empty space next to me where Sakeena had lain the night before. "Where is she?" I thought. I got up from the bed and wandered from the bedroom into the living room. There was dead silence in the house. I glanced over at the clock on the little table next to the couch. 7:51. "Damn, It's early as hell." I'm not usually awake this early. Then the smell of food came to me as I got closer to the kitchen. I walked into the kitchen to find a note on the fridge.

"Isaac' I hope that you slept well. I really enjoyed myself yesterday. I had to be at work early this morning but I left you something to eat in the oven. Hope to see you soon. Kisses, Keena."

Now that's the good shit that I'm talking about. I opened the oven door and found myself some good eating. She had made pancakes with scrambled eggs and cheese and turkey sausage. It was still warm. Which lead me to believe that she must not have left too long ago. I took a glass of orange juice and sat down on the couch. There were pictures of Sakeena and some other women on the coffee table in front of me. As I ate, I picked up the phone and called Sun's cell phone.

"Hello." He answered after the first ring.

"What's up Sun?"

"Isaac', is that your punk ass? Where you been? Khi and I have been looking for your ass all night. I know you have to be with a bitch if you're calling me this early."

"She's not a bitch," I replied dryly.

"You must be with that girl that Khi was telling me about. Did you fuck her? Please tell me that you fucked or at least got some jawbone."

I knew that I was about to get it when I answered. "Nah, we were just chillin."

"What?" He screamed into the phone. "What the fuck you mean chillin? What does that mean? Chillin, don't tell me that you're a rest haven for hoes now."

"Look man. I'm kinda feeling this girl. So can I live?" He didn't say anything. As a matter of fact, he hung up. When I called back, he answered the phone laughing.

"You're digging her and you didn't tap that ass? She had to do something to you. Did she blow in your butt with a straw?" He said jokingly.

"No fool. I just like her style. Listen I didn't call you to be yapping on the phone. Come get your boy and stop playing around." Sun was still laughing in the back ground when he replied.

"Alright nigga. Tell me how to get to your love palace?"

After I hung up the phone with Sun, I went back to the bedroom and sat down on the end of the bed. When I bent over to put my shoe on, I could still smell Sakeena's fragrance on my shirt. I straightened out the bed and went back into the living room and watched TV while I waited for Sun. When I heard the horn blow, I went to the window and looked between the blinds. It was Sun. But it wasn't Sun's car. The sunroof to the shiny cranberry colored 540i slid open with Sun's smiling face waiting behind it.

"Come on, ya nasty ass nigga, it's me!" He yelled as he started banging on the horn.

I locked the door from the inside and ran out to the car.

"Where she at?" he asked.

"She went to work," I said as I got into the car.

"Went to work? She left your stinking ass in her house alone and went to work? Damn. She got you acting like a bitch. You're supposed to leave her in the bed curled up only to awake to an empty bed."

"I don't think so. That's beside the point. Whose car is this?" He made a "come on now" face.

"You know how pimpin' do. Some chic I been messing around with on the down low. Check this out, I'm trying to set up a little thing with her and her girlfriend. Bitch got dough too! She's some kinda computer something. I don't know. But SHE GOT A FAT ASS!" He shouted.

Fat ass did sound like a good idea. "So what's up with her friend?"

He looked at me and smiled. "Now that's the Isaac' that I know. After I drop you off, I'm going to see shorty and set something up for tonight."

I pondered the thought for a minute. I really am getting tired of all this chasing women shit but, at this point my flesh is still weak. I honestly do want to try and slow down and maybe see what's up with Keena. But I don't think one more fiasco will kill me. "Alright. Just call me and let me know what's up."

After Sun dropped me off, I really needed some wind down time. First I'm going to call Sakeena and then I'll take it down. I picked up the phone and called. This time I didn't feel as nervous.

"Sakeena speaking."

"Hey you." I said in my cute voice.

"HEY!" She replied happily. "Did you like the breakfast that I made for you?"

"Most definitely. Thanks. But you could have waked me up. I wouldn't have minded."

"I didn't want to wake you. You looked so cute all curled up sleeping."

"Thank you," I said in my best baby voice. "I know that you're probably busy, but I wanted to hear your voice so I called." I could hear her smiling over the phone.

"Well thank you very much Mr. Jordan, I'll talk to you later ok."

After she hung up I checked my messages. Sada going crazy. Shawn trying to hook up later and a hand full of other silly bitches whining and moaning about the lack of time spent. I kicked my shoes off and climbed up onto my bed. As I lay back, I, for the first time started to think about all of the different women that I've slept with or at least tried to think about how they felt. Anyway, being the piece of shit that I am, I always thought about me. But never about them or how they felt. Lisa, Sada, Shawn and a bunch whose names I don't even remember. Lying here and reflecting, I've probably had sex with three or four hundred women. Some I've hurt with no regard to their feelings. I mean, I've had lots of one-night stands. But I've also had a lot of those long-term, no commitment type of relationships. You know the kind that includes everything that a real relationship has except that I'm running around fucking like a jackrabbit. For me, they were about the sex. I did like quite a few of them, but in the end it was about the sex. I know that it was about more than that for the few that I did like. It was about the hope that I might change. Change into a one woman man. I have longed for a steady woman for a long time, but I'm afraid. That may sound strange but it's true. I'm afraid that I might lose my freedom and myself. And besides, I like being free. But most of all, I'm afraid to lose my love. Like I said men like me are born and made. And even though I can't exactly relate to how they feel, I know what it feels like to be crushed by the weight of one's own heart. And that is what keeps me focused. I didn't like it when it happened to me and if I can help it, I'm damn sure not going to let it happen again. Thinking about how they must feel when that day comes when I say, "I don't want to deal with you anymore," is hard. I've seen lots of tears. Whether they were tears of anger or joy, they were still tears. And the longer that "The Game" goes on, the more that it hurts. Don't get me wrong, I know that it doesn't hurt me the same way that it hurts them. But it does hurt when I really think about it. Maybe it does hurt me more because I am only one person absorbing all the pain for a group of people. But it is pain that I've caused so I guess that's the price that I have to pay. Sometimes I really wish that I can change what I have done, but I know I can't. As I lay here in the dark, tears have built up on the insides of my lids and run down my face as I nod off to sleep. I try to dream about being with someone special. But unfortunately, my phone rings. It's Sun.

"Yo, Ike. What's up kid?"

"Didn't you just drop me off not too long ago? What do you think is up? I'm trying to get some rest."

"You know what I mean. What's up with later? I got the bitches," he replied.

"Sun, let me ask you a question?"

"Oh boy," he interrupted.

"Please don't get on none of that gay, sucker-for-love shit."

"Come on man! How long do you think you, me and Mekhi can run around fucking everyone that we see?" He paused for a few seconds.

"As long as I feel like my dick can take it," he said laughing.

"I'm serious Sun."

"Ok, ok. Look, I'm gonna go until I'm ready not to. It's just that simple. Ike, you're my man. But don't force it. In the long run, you'll regret it."

That was the first time that Sun said something that made sense in a long time. "I hear you," I said. But of course he interrupted.

"Are you fucking with me and these bitches or not?"

He sounded a little aggravated this time. Usually when the pack sees one of their own going astray, it tends to send out bad vibes. "Nah, I don't think so," I said slowly.

"Alright then, I'ma have to call Khi."

Before I could say anything, he hung up. I knew he was mad now. As I dozed back off, I thought about what my life would be like if I would have given just one of those women, the love and undivided attention that I could if I wasn't too afraid. Maybe I could have had a family and some babies. Maybe even a little house in the suburbs. Then again, I could be paying child support and alimony. In baseball, getting a hit fifty percent of the time will get you into the hall of fame. But in love, and in life, fifty-fifty just ain't the kind of odds that I want to bet on.

SATURDAY

Hopefully Saturday will be a good day. I must have been tired as hell last night because I didn't hear the phone ring all night. On top of that, I've slept in my clothes for the last two nights. I guess all that running around is finally starting to catch up with me. And at the ripe old age of twenty-five years old, I ain't no spring chicken. I roll over and wipe the sleep from my eyes as I push the button on the answering machine. Sada babbling. Shawn trying to hook up last night. Mekhi and Sun calling to tell me about the play by play of last night's activity and tell me that I'm acting like a bitch because I didn't want to be bothered with them and those chicks. And two other silly ass bitches that I met awhile ago. Last but far from least, there was a message from Keena. I leaned over and picked up the phone to call Mekhi. After about six rings, he finally answered.

"Mekhi, what the hell are you doing? What took you so long to answer the phone?"

"Yo kid," he whispered. "Sun and I had an orgy with those two bitches from last night and they're still here. Sun is in the bedroom with the both of them right now."

That surprised me a little. Usually the idea was to have whoever it was fucked and gone early. "Say word. Well I just called to see what's up for tonight. Are we still going out tonight or what?"

"Yeah, no doubt, I'll hit you later and let you know what's up."

"I'm thinking about inviting Keena, so get yourself a date." He didn't answer this time. "Mekhi?" When he did answer, he sounded distracted.

"Yo, I gotta go. I think you better call me later."

I figured that the festivities had begun to heat up again, so I hung up. Then I hit the speed dial for Keena.

"Hello Mr. Jordan, how are you this morning?"

Caller ID is the shit sometimes. "I'm fine. I'm sorry that I didn't answer when you called last night, but a brother was real tired and didn't even hear the phone ring."

"That's ok I understand. Sometimes we all get extremely tired. It's just up to us to listen when our bodies start talking."

This is scary. She's bad as hell, doing her own thing, and she's understanding. I gotta keep her even if I don't want to. "Well Ms. Thomas, I called to see if you would like to join me and some of my friends for a group outing this evening."

"If you don't mind me being around your friends."

I thought that was funny. "Of course I don't mind, I want to you to meet my boys, Mekhi and Sun."

"Ok. Where are we going?"

"Now that, I don't know just yet, but as soon as I find out, you will be the first to know." Before she could answer, the phone beeped. "Please hold," I said. When I clicked over, it was Shawn. As soon as I heard her voice, I flipped. "Are you fuckin crazy? I understand that we both know that we fuck other people, but why would your stupid ass tell somebody that you don't even know?" Her voice was high pitched when she spoke.

"I didn't know that you were telling her that she was wifey! You said that everyone you mess with knows that you're fuckin around with other people."

She didn't really believe that, did she? "Hold on stupid." I clicked back over and Keena was gone. "Dammit!" I yelled. As soon as I returned back to Shawn, she started babbling.

"Your girl is crazy. She said she was gonna fuck you up bad. And then she said she was going to do some stuff to your dick!"

"My dick? There is no way she's doing anything to my dick or me for that matter. I will knock her the fuck out if she run up on me with that dumb shit. Woman or no woman, I'ma muthafuckin' pimp and she will get her shit slapped back to the white meat!" I shouted.

"To the white meat? Huh? And you a pimp?" She laughed.

"No doubt!"

"How much of a pimp are you, daddy?" She said in her usual sexy tone.

"Enough of a pimp for your ass. "

"Well, why don't I come over and see."

I pondered that thought for a minute. I know that I said that.

I was tired of this. But I was still hype from the conversation that I needed to bust a quick nut. "Ok, how about three thirty?"

"Sounds like a date. I will definitely be there."

I hung up the phone and lay back with my arms above my head. "Why did I just do that?" I whispered to myself. I guess the flesh *is* weak. Now I have to call Keena back and tell her some lie to explain why I left her on hold for so long. I guess a simple lie will do, I shouldn't really need one of my specials. Keena answered the phone in her usually cheery voice.

"Hey! You couldn't wait to talk with me so you called again." She said jokingly.

"Yes, but I also wanted to apologize for leaving you on hold. I had to…"

"It's ok," she interrupted. "Whatever it was had to be important."

Cool, now I don't have to lie.

"If I said that I wanted to come and see you now, would you think that I was foolish?"

"No, of course not."

"Well, a girlfriend of mine doesn't live too far from you and I was going to be at her house and was wondering if I could stop by for a little while."

I liked the idea of that. "I would never turn down a visit from you." Classic brown nosing. "Just call me when you're on your way."

"Ok. Then I'll see you in a little while."

I hung up the phone and made a dash for the bathroom. I had to be presentable when Keena came. I haven't been this excited about a woman coming to see me in a while. Not since I first met the dumb bitch, who shall remain nameless, that ripped my heart out and left me to be what I am today. Now that I think about it, she couldn't have been that stupid if she fooled me. I must be the dumb ass. All that doesn't matter now because Keena has awakened something inside of me that has been dead and buried for a long time. She caused me to think about things that most guys like me don't think about. She has me thinking about growing old alone. And as soft as it may sound, even I don't want that. You tend not to think about it when you're out there doing your thing. But if you meet someone that could be special, you start to wonder if there is a light at the seemingly endless tunnel of pussy. Dying old and alone is something that I do not want to do, under no circumstances. It is a very pathetic thought. And these few days with her have bought that to light.

"Oh Shit!" I yelled as I got out of the shower. I forgot all about Shawn, who I could see from the bathroom window walking up to my house. I grabbed a towel and ran back into my bedroom. I picked up the phone and dialed Shawn's cell phone number.

"Hello? Isaac, why are you calling me when I am right outside of your house?"

"I was trying to catch you at your house before you left. I'm gonna have to take a rain check. I have something important to do." There was dead air.

"I bet you do you fuckin whore! You have another bitch coming over! Don't you?"

That was pretty impressive I thought. "What I am doing is beside the point...I just can't fuck with you right now."

"So what if I stayed out here in front of your house for a while?"

"Come on Shawn. Now you're acting like Sada. I thought that your shit was tight and that you don't get all bent outta shape over men."

She paused before answering. "Yeah, you right, but a sista was ready to do her thing and you bull-shittin me for a new bitch that you might not fuck. My pussy is guaranteed."

This was true but that first statement pissed me off. "First of all, she ain't no bitch. And second of all, last I heard, this is my dick and I can do what the fuck I want with it. So you can stand out there if you want, but you ain't coming in here."

"Fuck you!" she said and hung up.

When I went to the window, I could see Shawn walking away mad as hell. "Oh well, she's a trick ass bitch anyway." I thought. I was slipping on a pair of jeans when the phone rang.

"Hey you, I should be there in about ten minutes."

A smile came over my face. "I'll be waiting."

When Keena arrived, I went out onto the porch to greet her. She had on some jeans and a snug t-shirt. I led her into the living room and pulled two chairs face to face.

"So do you know where we are going tonight?"

"I'm still not sure yet, I'm still waiting to hear from my boys."

Just the fact that we were sitting face to face had my heart racing a hundred miles an hour. The more that we talked, the closer we got until we were right in each others' face. I guess now is as good as a time as any. I took Keena's hands and pulled her towards me. Our eyes met one last time before our lips met. When we kissed, the smell of her surrounded us. It wasn't a sickening smell like that other dumb bitch Kamila, it was different. Her kiss had a calming effect on me. Our tongues did a forbidden dance. The steel ball in her tongue glided along the underside of my tongue with ease. She squeezed my hands tightly as pulled away from me. She gasped as she sat back I in the chair. The silence seemed so loud now.

"I'm sorry, I shouldn't have done that," I said in a childlike tone.

81

"It's ok, if I didn't want to do it, I wouldn't have let you. It was nice though." She said smiling.

We sat for a moment gazing into each other's eyes. The silence was broken by the sudden ringing of the phone.

"Hello."

"What's the deal my nigga?" Mekhi's voice came over the phone like a loud speaker. "What are you doin?"

"I'm just chillin with Sakeena," I replied dryly. I knew that he was about to start trippin. CHILLIN' WITH SAKEENA? Don't you think you're going a little overboard with this trying to chill out shit?"

I didn't like what he said, not because of what he said, but because I always let Mekhi do him with no questions asked. So why was he fuckin with me? I couldn't understand.

"Yo Ike, don't pay that nigga no mind," Sun's voice stepped in on the three way call. "He's just mad because you doin your thing with shorty and he's still fuckin with those stank ass hoes."

I like the fact that Sun was a firm believer of "Do what you like and as long as you like it, fuck everybody else." He never judges what you do as long as it makes you happy. "Anyway, what's the deal for tonight? Where are we gonna go?"

"I think we should hit the Spy Bar down on Greene Street in Soho," Mekhi said.

"I'm with that, we haven't been there in a while."

"Then it's on. Spy Bar it is. I still got the Beemer so we can meet up and bounce around ten," Sun said.

"Alright then, we'll meet at Isaac's house at ten."

I hung up the phone and looked into Sakeena's eyes for an indication of what to do. She smiled at me.

"I take it that you know where we are going tonight."

"Yeah, we're going to this place out in the city called Spy Bar. We're all going to meet here at ten. Can you make it?"

"I most certainly can. Can I bring my girlfriend? She needs to get out."

"Sure." I said as I stood up from the chair. "Just make sure you're here. I wouldn't want to miss out on what I just had." The way I looked at her let her know that I wanted her in a bad way. And telling from her look, she felt the same way.

"Well, I'm going to get back to my girl's house and rest up for tonight. I'll see you later."

I led her to the door and opened it. As she went out, I grabbed her arm and turned her back around towards me. I took her close and kissed her gently on the lips. "See you later," I said slowly. She went out to the car and got in. As she drove off, she looked back and smiled. Now all I have to do is wait for tonight. I think I'm gonna stay in and watch TV to keep myself from getting into trouble. I went back into my bedroom, turned on the TV and laid down. Slowly, I felt myself drift off to sleep. Hopefully, my slumber will be filled with dreams of Keena.

ISAAC

I awoke to the sounds of the alarm clock feeling as if it was a new day. The time that I had spent with Sakeena earlier had rejuvenated me. That and the fact that I finally got some real sleep helped. It was eight forty five. That gives me plenty of time to get ready before everyone starts showing up. I showered and started getting ready. I went into my silk specials drawer of boxers. "Mmm, let's see, what will I go with? Maybe the ones with the little hot tamales on them? Nah! I know. The ones with the wolfs head on the front so in case something good happens, Keena will know that I'm hungry like a wolf for her." I sang. Of course I had to put the smell goods in all the right places. You know how I do. I went over to my closet and pulled out this black DKNY suit that I've been waiting to use for evil. The Kenny Cole slippery shoes are definitely gonna hurt 'em. As soon as I got my clothes on, the phone rang.

"We out front nigga," Mekhi barked into the phone.

I went outside to find Mekhi laced in all black with his toes out. Sun had on another one of those tight ass muscle shirts. "Damn Sun. Did you just finish doing some pushups?" I joked.

"Man fucks y'all. Mekhi was just fuckin with me about my shirt too."

I saw a head moving around in the car so I figured that it was the owner. I went over to the car and knocked on the window. "How you doin? My names Isaac and you are?" I said extending my hand.

"Tasha." The dark chocolate sweetness replied.

"Nice car."

"Thanks, but it's not mine."

No this guy did not pick up another girl in ol' girl's car. "Oops, my bad.

"You ain't bullshitting." Sun's suddenly heated voice said.

"You are slipping my man," Mekhi sang out loud. "Yo, where's your girl at?"

"She should be here any minute." Right on cue the same car that Keena had been driving earlier turned the corner. This time, there was another young lady driving. I was sure it was the owner. When the car stopped, Keena got out and walked around the car. As she stepped from behind the car, it was over. She was dressed in a spaghetti strapped one-piece black dress that climbed a touch above her mid thigh and a pair of banging ass open-toed shoes.

"She's bad as hell," Mekhi mumbled under his breath.

"You ain't never lied," Sun agreed.

As she walked towards us, Sun came up next to me.

"Hey baby," she said as she kissed me on the cheek.

"What's up lady? Sakeena this is Mekhi and Sun," I said, motioning to them both. "Mekhi, Sun this is Sakeena."

After they exchanged pleasantries, we went over to Keena's ride and introduced ourselves. Her name was Mina. I found that rather amusing Sakeena, Mina, you know? Mekhi had that predator look in his eyes. Since he decided to go solo tonight, if all else failed, she was there. Shorty was tight. She was a browned skinned sister with shoulder length locks. From where I was standing, she seemed like she had a nice little body. I rode in the car with Sakeena and Mina, while Sun headed off with Mekhi and Tasha. We arrived in the city in no time. The line at Spy was its usual blend of ethnicity. Asian, White, Black, Hispanic, all the colors of the rainbow. There was a mass of blackness and shadows as we entered. I took Sakeena's hand and led her and the rest of our entourage to the back of the club. We sat down on the huge couches that lined the back wall. The waitress came over and took all of our orders. We sat and talked for a while when one of my many songs came on. "There She Goes," by Babyface. It blew through the speakers as I leaped up from my seat pulling Sakeena behind me.

"That's my shit!" I yelled as we moved to the middle of the dance floor. Keena turned her back to me and pressed her body against mine. Again her scent engulfed me and drew me closer to her. Our bodies moved to the rhythm of each other. "Damn, she feels so good," I thought to myself. Everything just seemed so clear now. I had made up my mind right then and there that I wasn't going to be alone anymore. As we spun around on the dance floor, I could see Mekhi and Sun making their way through the crowd with Tasha and Mina in tow. As Mekhi approached me he mouthed the words, "Our drinks are here." Then suddenly a frown came over his face as he looked over my shoulder. When I turned to see what he was looking at, my heart almost jumped out of my chest when I saw Shawn and Sada, standing not more than ten feet away from us. When I looked into Shawn's face, she had a bit of a smirk, but when I looked at Sada I could see the fire and hatred in her eyes. Everything seemed to be moving in slow motion. I've been caught up in some shit before, but nothing like this.

"You thought I wasn't gonna catch up to your ass didn't you? You piece of shit," Sada screamed. "And who the fuck is this? Another one of your bitches?"

"Who the fuck are you calling a bitch?" Sakeena's face turned bright red as she moved towards Sada. I grabbed Keena's arm and pulled her back towards me.

"What the fuck is wrong with you? You stupid bitch!" Mekhi screamed.

By now the crowd started to part like the red sea. Now everything was happening too fast. "I have to get this under control," I thought to myself.

"Sada! Are you crazy running up on me in public like this?"

The whole time Shawn just stood and watched with that stupid smirk on her face. In the distance, I could see the big ass security guards coming. I took a step towards Sada with my arm extended. She jumped back, reached into her purse and pulled out a nickel-plated 9mm. The combination of the darkness of the crowd and the shininess of the burner made it seem as if she had just pulled the sun out of the sky.

"SHE'S GOTTA GUN!" Someone yelled out, sending the entire club into total chaos. Everyone scattered! Telling by the look on Shawn's face, this was not part of the plan. Amazing to me, when Shawn saw the gun she reached out and grabbed Sada's arm, but the anger of Sada far outweighed the fear of Shawn. Sada shoved Shawn to the floor and raised the chrome steel in Sakeena's and my direction.

"I told you that you weren't gonna hurt no one else you bastard!"

I pushed Sakeena in Mekhi's direction as I saw the fire coming from between Sada's hands. I couldn't hear anything. I saw about three or four flashes of light, then everything and everyone was moving in slow motion. The sudden burn of fire in my chest brought everything back to normal speed. I staggered back into Sun's arms and slumped to the floor. My shirt was soaked in my own blood. I tried to get up, but my entire knee was blown apart. As Sun laid me on the floor, I could see security wrestling Sada to the floor. Her eyes were fixated on mine and the hatred had now turned to sorrow.

"SOMEONE CALL A FUCKING AMBULANCE!" Sun yelled over the music.

I could see Keena reaching for me screaming as Mekhi held her tightly around her waist. People were running everywhere. I could feel my heart beating faster than it had ever before. Now everything was moving fast, like it does when you fast-forward a VCR while the movie is still on the screen. I started to remember so many things. I remembered my mother's womb, I remembered the time that I fell from the tree outside of my grandmother's house and broke my arm. I remembered my mom, my dad. I remembered my first day of grammar school. I remembered freshman year, when little Annie Caves let me touch her butt in the alley behind the football field in high school. She was holding like a grown ass woman. I remembered the first time that I met Mekhi and Sun. Sun looked so funny back in the day with his high top fade, it sat on his head like a hamburger. I saw a lot of the faces of the women that I've done dirty over the years ending with Sada. I saw Sakeena again, the day when we first met. My saving angel. I opened my eyes to see Sun holding his hands over the smoking holes in my chest. I could feel the blood overflowing from my lungs into my throat and mouth. Sakeena and Mekhi were kneeling down beside me and Keena's eyes were filled with tears.

"COME ON MAN, STAY WITH ME, DON'T YOU LEAVE ME!" Mekhi shouted as I took Keena and his hands in mine.

Sun placed his hand on top of ours and we all squeezed tight, feeling the failing beat of my heart was something that I could never have imagined. Slowly I could feel my body becoming cold and stiff as my life force was being drained out of me, which wasn't the worst thing in the world because I guess I finally got my biggest wish. Maybe it came too soon and maybe it came in the form of karma coming back for me with a vengeance, but I didn't die alone.

ACKNOWLEDGMENTS

BIAN

AUTHOR'S NOTE

For a further look into the Author go to
www.xplorefreedom.com
www.facebook.com/xplorefreedom

Provocative books with strong themes and even stronger writing.

FOCUS WRITE INPSIRE PUBLISHING

Check out

www.facebook.com/focuswriteinspire.llc

for author interviews,

questions for discussion,

trailers, and more!

 ® Focus Write Inspire.LLC Newark NJ (USA)

FOCUS WRITE INSPIRE PUBLISHING
Also brings you

FOCUS WRITE INSPIRE PUBLISHING
Also brings you

Made in the USA
Charleston, SC
16 January 2014